Adapted by Jim Pascoe

Based on the series created by

Mark McCorkle & Bob Schooley

New York

S0-AUB-140

Copyright © 2004 Disney Enterprises, Inc.

All rights reserved. No part of this book may be reproduced
or transmitted in any form or by any means, electronic or
mechanical, including photocopying, recording, or by any
information storage and retrieval system, without written
permission from the publisher. For information address
Disney Press, 114 Fifth Avenue, New York, New York 10011-5690.

Printed in the United States of America

First Edition
1 3 5 7 9 10 8 6 4 2

Library of Congress Catalog Card Number: 2003105737

ISBN 0-7868-4612-7

For more Disney Press fun, visit www.disneybooks.com
Visit DisneyChannel.com

If you purchased this book without a cover, you should be aware
that this book is stolen property. It was reported as "unsold and
destroyed" to the publisher, and neither the author nor the
publisher has received any payment for this "stripped" book.

CHAPTER 1

Cheer Leader

Saving the world without a driver's license? No big, thought Kim Possible. But this? This was a challenge. This was cheerleading practice!

As Kim struggled to the top of the human pyramid, the cheerleaders clapped out a funky rhythm. "M-A-D! D-O-G! That's how we spell vic-to-ry! Go, Mad Dogs! Go, go, Mad Dogs! Go, Mad Dogs! Go, go, Mad Dogs!"

"We're number one!" Kim cried, putting

every last bit of energy into the cheer. Then she jumped off the pyramid's top, flipped around, and landed with a perfect split. This was the kind of awesome move that had made Kim cheerleader captain.

"Okay. Great practice, team!" Kim called to her fellow cheerleaders. The group gathered their things and filed out of the Middleton High gym.

"Kim . . . can we chat?" Bonnie Rockwaller said in her usual sweet-and-sour way. Bonnie was Kim's rival. She was also way perfect—in her own mind!

Kim was *so* not looking forward to dealing with Bonnie. But Kim was team captain. So she forced herself to face Bonnie and say, "Sure, Bonnie. I have time for anyone on the squad. What's your ish?"

Bonnie took Kim by the arm. "Well, it's really *your* ish. You seem . . . tired."

"I did fly in from Abu Dhabi this morning. Rescued an ambassador," Kim said proudly.

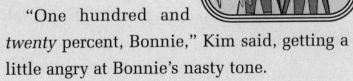

"Which is nice. But you've gotta ask yourself: did you give the squad one hundred and ten percent today?"

"One hundred and *twenty* percent, Bonnie," Kim said, getting a little angry at Bonnie's nasty tone.

"I happen to think the squad deserves a captain who gives, like . . . one hundred and *thirty* percent," Bonnie said smugly.

Kim was starting to get the picture. "Someone like—"

"Me," Bonnie said, pointing to herself.

"Look, if you want to make a play for cap-tain, take it to the squad," Kim said. "If they want Bonnie instead of Kim, super for Bonnie."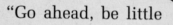

"Go ahead, be little Miss Smug-mug, but I *will* be squad captain," Bonnie snapped.

Kim fumed. Fighting supervillains really *was* no big compared to a high school headache like this!

After practice, Kim found her best friend, Ron Stoppable, at their usual after-school hangout, Bueno Nacho.

"I can't believe this," Kim said in one long groan.

"Believe it, K.P. They're cutting back on the beans." Ron squinted at his burrito.

Kim sighed. She was talking about *Bonnie*, not burritos. Sitting in the booth across from Ron, she waited for him to get serious.

Ron reached into his pocket and pulled out his pet naked mole rat. Rufus, half asleep, gave a big yawn.

"Rufus," Ron said, "I want an analysis of this burrito. Stat!"

Rufus's eyes popped open. *Mmm-yumm-mmm.*

"Nothing invasive," Ron told him. "Just take a look around. I want a cheese-bean ratio."

Lifting up the tortilla with

his paw, Rufus crawled inside the burrito.

Kim drummed her fingers on the table. This was *not* the kind of serious talk she had in mind when she sat down. "Ron, have you been listening to a word I've said?"

Ron straightened up and did his best Kim Possible impersonation: "'Bonnie has the nerve to challenge me after all I've done for

the squad? After all I've done for her! I can't believe this.' Close quote."

Kim took an annoyed slurp of soda. Ron had gotten her good. Talk about humiliation nation!

"Now," he said, "were *you* listening to *my* burrito problem?"

A huge burp ripped through Bueno Nacho. Ron looked down to see where the burp had come from.

"Hey!" Ron cried.

Rufus's belly was bulging out. The naked mole rat gave Ron a thumbs-up. "Good burrito," Rufus mumbled.

Then Rufus groaned and fell back on the plastic tray, his little tongue hanging from his little mouth.

Ron ordered another burrito. After he had finished gulping it down, Kim and Ron left the restaurant, and Kim continued talking about the *real* problem: Bonnie Rockwaller.

"Bonnie's just wasting her time," Kim said. "She doesn't stand a chance."

"Be careful, Kim. She's tricky," Ron said

as he walked on ahead of her. "Expect it to get dirty."

Suddenly, a hole in the ground opened up right below where Kim was walking. *Whoosh!* Kim fell through, and just as suddenly, the hole closed up again.

Ron heard Kim cry out. He looked all around, completely confused. "Kim?" he asked. But no one answered. She was gone.

CHAPTER 2

A New Mission

P*lop!* Kim dropped down from the mysterious hole in the sidewalk. She found herself trapped inside a strange glass capsule. As she got to her feet, she heard a door shut above her.

"Hey!" she yelled.

Swoosh! The tiny glass capsule dropped like a speeding elevator. It carried her underground through a maze of green tubes. *Zig!* Her tube turned to the right. *Zag!* It turned to

11

the left. *Whoosh!* It did a loop-the-loop—then it zoomed straight down.

Finally, it stopped. And Kim was *not* happy.

"Let me out!" Kim pounded on the glass walls. "Let me"— suddenly, the glass in front of her slid open—"out!"

She tumbled free. Face-first.

"Okay . . ." she said, looking all around, "what's the sitch?"

A woman with an eye patch stepped in front of her. "Kim Possible. Welcome."

Kim didn't recognize the woman. She had short, dark hair and wore a skintight blue uniform with black boots.

"Welcome to where?" Kim asked as she stood up.

"To the Global Justice Network," said the woman.

"G.J.? No way!" Kim couldn't believe it. She'd always admired their crime-fighting work.

"Affirmative way," said the woman. "I'm Dr. Director, the head of G.J."

Whoosh! Kim spun around to see another green tube arrive and open up. Out walked a boy. He was Kim's age and dressed in a blue uniform like Dr. Director's. He would have been cute if the look on his face hadn't been so serious.

"This is Will Du, our *number-one* agent," said Dr. Director. Then to both of them she said, "Follow me."

The two teenagers stared

at each other. Will raised an eyebrow. And Kim
breezed past, thinking, Who *is* this guy and
what's *his* ish?

Kim and Will Du sat down next to Dr.
Director at a huge table. Three huge projector
screens hung above them.

"This is Professor Sylvan Green," said Dr.
Director, flicking a button on a remote control. An image of the professor flashed on all
three screens. He was a young, gawky man
with big ears, sandy brown hair, and glasses.

The head of G.J. continued: "In the 1960s
he developed a top-secret missile defense
project."

"The Sirenita guided-missile tracking system," Kim said.

Dr. Director looked shocked—that was top secret stuff! "Where did you get that information?"

Kim shrugged. "Off the Web."

"Oh. Ah." Dr. Director cleared her throat. She continued with another click of the remote.

"This is Professor Green, currently." A new image showed a man with the same glasses and the same big ears. Only now his hair was gone, and he was sitting on a goofy

riding lawn mower. "Retired. Place of residence: Florida."

"But now he's disappeared," Kim said.

Dr. Director sighed. "Yes. Was that on the Internet, too?"

"No," Kim told her. "That was a guess."

"Kim," said Dr. Director, "what would you say to helping Agent Du find Professor Green?"

Kim glanced at Agent Will Du. He looked like he'd be about as much fun as math class. "Does Agent Du talk?"

"Fourteen languages. Thirty-two regional dialects," Agent Du responded.

"That's cool. I'm taking French." Kim turned to Dr. Director. "Ah, you know this is a ferociously bad time for me. There's this girl at school, a major 'all that' type, and really I—"

"Dr. Director, permission to speak freely," Will said, scowling.

"Granted," his boss said.

"This is an insult!" Will cried. "I am a highly trained professional. And she's . . . she's . . . an *amateur*!"

First Bonnie, now this guy, Kim thought, annoyed. Challenges were piling up everywhere!

"Okay. I'm in," she told them.

Will Du sneered. But he didn't say another word.

Dr. Director smiled. "Kim Possible, Agent Du . . . good luck."

CHAPTER 3

A Truckload of Trouble

"**M**an, I thought for sure Bonnie had taken you out of the picture," Ron said to Kim after school the next day. They were walking out the front entrance of Middleton High.

"Oh, please," Kim said. "You know, she didn't even show up for practice."

"Miss Possible . . ." Kim and Ron stopped when they heard the unfriendly voice. It was Will Du. "Are you ready to assist me in *my* investigation?" he asked smugly.

"*Assist* you? No," Kim told him. "*Work with you as an equal?* Sure."

Ron thought he'd better check out this Will Du dude. He decided to start with the friendly approach. "Yoha-broha!" he said with a wave of his hand.

Agent Du reacted like he was being attacked. He tapped a button on the face of his watch. A wire shot out of the timepiece and attached itself to Ron's chest.

Zappo! An electric shock ran through Ron. He collapsed in a heap.

Kim rushed over to help. She yelled at Will, "What did you do to him?!"

"Stopwatch. Temporary paralysis," Will said with total calm. "Standard procedure for anyone who comes within one meter of my person."

19

Kim reached into Ron's cargo pants pocket and pulled out Rufus. Ron's naked mole rat was stiff as a stick!

"Oh, poor Rufus," Kim said.

Now Agent Du began to *talk* into his watch. Apparently, it was also a voice recorder. "Note: subject appears to keep hairless rodent in pant pocket."

This boy was getting Kim totally tweaked. She waved the stiff Rufus by his tail right in Will's face. "His name is Rufus, and he's a naked mole rat, Mister-I-Know-Everything."

"Ahhh . . . *Heterocephalus glaber*," Will babbled into his watch.

Ron sprang to his feet, wide awake. Time for take two. "Yoha-broha!" he said again.

Will jumped back into a martial arts pose.

"*Wha-ha!*" Ron's arms flew wildly around. "Right back atcha, dude!" he cried.

Kim placed Rufus into Ron's hand. "Come on, you two."

As she moved past the boys, Kim saw Bonnie Rockwaller walking toward her.

"Hi, K.," Bonnie sang with totally fake cheeriness.

"Missed you at practice, B.," Kim sang right back.

"I had to launch our new fund-raiser,"

Bonnie said as she handed Kim a purple box.

Kim looked at the strange box in her hands. "What fund-raiser?"

"I know your *world-saving* keeps you busy and all," Bonnie said. "But do you think maybe *you* can sell a box?"

"Oh, chocolates." Kim pulled out a bar. "Oh, I could sell a box. Easy."

"Super!" Bonnie said.

Just then, a horn blared loudly from the school parking lot. Bonnie turned and walked over to a huge truck. It was filled with chocolate bars!

"Hoping to sell a few myself," said Bonnie.

A few? thought Kim. There must have been *thousands* of bars in there!

Bonnie hopped into the truck. "Later," she said. Then the huge candy rig drove off.

"You know, she's only kidding herself," Kim said to Ron and Will. "There is no way she's gonna sell all that. Let's just get on with the mission."

Ron grabbed her by the arm. "Wait, K.P. Am I the only one taking the Bonnie problem seriously?"

Kim waved her hand like *whatever*. "Oh, the Bonnie problem is really no big."

"Kim, we cannot ignore the chocolate challenge," Ron said.

"We?" she asked.

"I'm here for you. Use me," said Ron.

"As what?" asked Kim.

He grabbed the candy box from her. "I am a natural-born

seller. I have the gift of gab. Here, allow me to demonstrate."

This, Kim thought, she would *have* to see.

Salesman Stoppable walked up to Will. Agent Du stood typically solid and unblinking. "Good day, sir," Ron began. "You look like a gentleman who enjoys the finer things in life. And what could be better than one point nine ounces of rich, creamy chocolate?"

Will just stared.

"I got plain? Crispy? Peanut?" Ron looked frantically in the box for the perfect bar to tempt Agent Will Du.

"Mac-a-da-mi-a," Ron teased, but Will still gave no response.

Ron stomped back over to Kim. "That's a

bad example," he growled. "No one can sell to *that* stiff."

Rufus grabbed a candy bar and scampered over to the grim agent.

Will stared at the naked mole rat. Then he handed over a dollar for the chocolate.

Waving the money in the air, Rufus squealed, "Whooo!"

"Except him," said Ron with a shrug. "But he's naked."

CHAPTER 4

A Plan Comes Together

Later that afternoon, Kim, Ron, and Will went over to Kim's house to discuss their mission.

"Hi, Kimmie," said Kim's mom, walking into the kitchen. "Who's your new friend?"

Will jumped up from the kitchen table and bowed. "Agent Will Du, ma'am. It's an honor to meet you, Dr. Possible."

Kim's mom put her hand to her chest in surprise. "You know me?"

"Your recent paper on the application of lasers in subcranial exploration was fascinating," Will said in his most respectful suck-up voice. "And  the photograph did not do you justice."

Dr. Possible whispered to her daughter, "Invite him over more often."

Mothers! Kim thought. "Mom, I've got to find a missing scientist."

"Good luck, Kimmie," Dr. Possible said as she left the room. "Have fun, kids."

Kim whipped out her Kimmunicator and set it on the table. The Kimmunicator was like a cell phone and supercomputer put together.

On the screen, the face of her friend Wade appeared. Wade was the ten-year-old genius who helped Kim and Ron on all of their world-saving missions.

"Wade, did you get the data?" Kim asked.

"Got it," Wade responded. "A holographic simulation of the missing professor's home."

With a *click* and *whir*, a tiny lens popped out of the Kimmunicator. It projected the see-through hologram onto the entire table.

"Cool!" Ron said. "Hey, Rufus, Wade's gone 3-D!"

Rufus hopped onto the table and started strolling through the holo-house. "Hmmmmmmm," he said, looking for a place to kick back. He found a comfy chair, and jumped into the air, hoping to land on it. But *bam!* He landed on his naked mole rat rear instead.

Will sneered. He thought this was a waste of time. "I've already examined the crime scene," he snapped.

Kim snapped back. "I haven't. Wade, enlarge the point of entry."

The hologram dissolved all around Rufus, who cried, "Waaahh!" in shock. It then projected a close-up of the side of the house. A large hole was blasted in the wall!

"Explosive method of entry. What's that?" Kim pointed her finger into the hologram at a tiny white speck.

"Can't tell," Wade said. "I'll isolate and

enlarge." His fingers flew across the keyboard in front of him.

The white speck grew larger and floated above the table.

"Good," Kim said. "Now, let's try to fill in the blanks."

"Running extrapolation routine." Wade kept typing at superspeed. His computer program drew a picture of what the white speck used to be.

It was a golf ball.

"A golf ball?" Ron asked.

"Professor Green was retired," Will added. "Many retired people golf."

Kim shut off the hologram and picked up the Kimmunicator. "Wade, does Professor Green show up in any online discussion groups?"

"Oh, yeah." Wade read

from his monitor. "Gardening, botany, experimental fertilizers. His lawn won the bluegrass ribbon three years in a row."

"Good-bye, Wade," Will said as he reached over and shut off the Kimmunicator. "This is pointless. The man was obviously captured for his weapon-system expertise."

"He was a weapons expert in the sixties," Kim said. "You could look up what he knows in the library."

Will headed for the door. "Working with an amateur is clearly a waste of my time," he said.

Kim smiled big. She knew something Will

didn't. "I haven't even told you about the other trace element I detected at the scene."

Will stopped. "What is it?"

"Hyperactic acid. An experimental fertilizer. Black market only." Kim winked at Ron. She knew she was one step ahead of Will.

Ron could see a plan coming together. "Sounds like we need to visit the world headquarters for black-market gardening supplies," he said. Then he looked around, confused, and asked, "Which would be *where*?"

CHAPTER 5

Cloak-and-Dagger Café

The desert marketplace was dark and dusty. Clay pots lined the empty alley. The only light came from a shadowy café. Kim Possible stepped up to the entrance. Ron and Will followed.

"If it's illegal, they sell it here," Kim said in a low voice. The place reeked of danger.

Ron didn't recognize the reek. He whipped out a bunch of chocolate bars. "Forget sellers," he said. "We need buyers.

33

Ya gotta move this merchandise if you're gonna keep up with Bonnie."

"Bonnie is *so* not a threat," Kim said. "C'mon."

The inside of the Cloak-and-Dagger Café smelled like strange spiced coffee. Men in red fez hats sat on velvet pillows and talked in hushed voices. In the far corner, on the biggest pillow, sat the biggest man.

"That's Big Daddy Brotherson," Kim told the others. "Every deal that goes down has his fingerprints all over it."

"Those are some *big* fingers," Ron said as he watched the huge, sweaty man chew on some grapes and spit out the seeds.

Will Du pushed Kim and Ron aside. "Excuse me, amateurs." He marched boldly across the room.

"Are you Big Daddy?" Will asked.

The fat man smiled a greasy smile. "That depends."

"I've got no time for games." Will held up his fist.

"That's too bad," Big Daddy said. "I was going to suggest you and my friend play *Thud*."

Will swallowed hard, then said, "Thud?"

Big Daddy clapped his big hands together. He was still smiling.

Out of the shadows came a huge gorilla of a bouncer. Unlike Big Daddy, he was *not* smiling.

Kim watched as the bouncer bounced Will across the room and through the window. He landed on the ground with a *thud*! "Ow," he whimpered.

Big Daddy's fat jiggled as he chuckled. "I love that game," he said.

"And I love it when I find out what I need to know"—Kim stepped close to Big Daddy—"like, who's been in the market for hyperactic acid?"

Big Daddy frowned at Kim. "Miss, we have one rule in this establishment: client confidentiality."

Kim pulled out a fund-raiser candy bar and waved it under his nose. He licked his big lips.

"Is that milk chocolate?" he asked.

Kim could hear his stomach growl!

"With chewy nougat," she answered with a sly smile.

Outside the café, Will and Ron waited for Kim. When she finally walked out, she struck a confident pose. "Duff Killigan," she said proudly.

Ron's eyes got big. "Who's that?"

Will pulled out his handheld computer. "My G.J. mobile database will tell us all about Killigan. Standard issue for all *top* agents."

Kim pulled out *her* handheld computer. "Kimmunicator. Extra special. Just for me."

Kim and Will furiously pushed buttons on their devices. They began reading the info as soon as it appeared on-screen. The data duel was on!

Kim said, "Duff Killigan. Born: Scotland."

"Former professional golfer," Will shot back.

Ron noticed a man standing on a nearby rooftop. He looked like he was holding a golf club.

"Ah . . . guys?" Ron said.

Will ignored Ron. "Banned from every golf course in the world. Even miniature golf."

"For excessive displays of temper," Kim countered, also ignoring Ron.

With a swing of his club, the golfer on the roof smacked a ball straight toward them. Ron yelled, "Guys!"

But Kim and Will were too busy data dueling.

"Weapon of choice—" Kim started.

"Exploding golf balls," Will finished.

Plop! The golf ball landed at their feet. Kim noticed that this particular golf ball was making a noise.

Beep, beep, beep, then (unfortunately) . . . *KABOOM!*

CHAPTER 6

Two Problems Equal a Whole Lotta Tweaked!

Luckily, just before the golf ball exploded, Ron pulled Kim and Will to safety in a marketplace alley.

Suddenly, Ron had a moment of panic. Where was his little whiskered friend? "Rufus, you okay?" he asked, pulling up the flap of his pants pocket.

Out popped the naked mole rat, a chocolate bar in his paw. *Chomp!* "Okay!" he squealed.

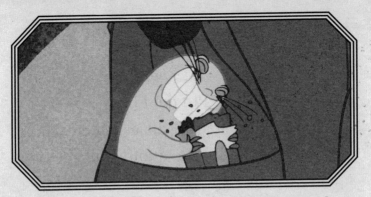

"Hey!" Ron cried, spying the chocolate. "You're paying for that!"

Suddenly, Will Du had a bright idea. "It all fits. The exploded golf ball at the crime scene. The attack on us. Killigan's our man."

"Gee, ya think?" Kim said. She rolled her eyes and pulled out the Kimmunicator. "Wade, we're after a rogue golfer named Duff Killigan. We need a location on his lair."

On-screen, Wade scratched his head. "Did you say 'rogue golfer'?"

"I know," Kim said. "Weird." She clicked off the Kimmunicator and spoke to Will and Ron. "Okay, I'm gonna go back to Middleton. See if Bonnie's sold any of *her* chocolate."

Kim stood in the Middleton High gym. Her jaw almost dropped to the floor.

"You sold them all?" she asked, shocked.

Bonnie smiled. "To quote our previous squad captain: 'No big.'"

"I'm not 'previous' yet," Kim snapped.

A bunch of the other cheerleaders stepped up behind Bonnie.

"Thanks to Bonnie, we got new uniforms!" said a blond cheerleader named Tara. "Aren't they badical!"

Bonnie tossed a new uniform in Kim's

face. "Better suit up, Kim. We're working on our new cheer."

"Don't tell me what to do," Kim said. "Wait, what new cheer?"

"Mine," Bonnie said.

Kim wrinkled her nose and said to herself, "Bonnie does not work this hard. Something is up."

Meanwhile, Will and Ron were sitting in a booth at Bueno Nacho.

"Hey, Will, watch this," Ron said. He held up his burrito and squeezed. *Splursh!* The bean-and-cheese insides shot straight up in the air. Ron put his face under the falling food and caught it in one sloppy bite. *Glomp!*

"Pretty cool, huh?" Ron said.

"If by 'cool' you mean utterly repulsive,"

Will said with a frown, "then yes. Quite cool, indeed."

Rufus wanted to get in on the action. He stomped on a nacho chip. *Splursh!* The cheese went up in the air. *Glomp!* He caught it in his little mole rat mouth.

"Nice one!" Ron said to Rufus.

Will just stared at them.

"So, can I ask you a question?" said Ron.

Will sighed. "If you must."

"Do you do normal stuff? Like go to school?" Ron asked.

"I am tutored by some of the world's greatest minds," said Will proudly.

"Tutored, huh?" Ron said. "No shame in that. Even I needed a little extra help in math freshman year."

"It is not because I'm remedial," Will said.

"Dude, it's *cool*," said Ron.

"You obviously don't understand—"

The beeping Kimmunicator cut Will off. Ron pulled it out of his pocket. "That'll be Wade," he said. "Better get Kim."

"I'm not remedial!" Will insisted, banging the table with his fists. Ron walked away.

* * *

Meanwhile, back in the school's gym, Bonnie finished her new cheer and leaped over to Kim. "In case you were wondering, Kim, that's what giving one hundred and *fifty* per-

cent looks like."

"Careful there, Bonnie," Kim said, annoyed. "I hear when you hit one hundred and *sixty* percent, you spontaneously combust."

Ron ran through the doorway. "K.P., we got a location on Duff Killigan."

Bonnie smiled. "Don't worry, Kim. *I'll* handle everything here."

Kim gritted her teeth. She was so tweaked, Ron could almost see the steam coming out of her ears.

She grabbed Ron by the shirt and stomped out. "Let's go," she grunted.

But even after Kim changed into her crime-fighting clothes, her mind was still on cheerleading practice.

"Bonnie is not this good. How could she have come up with that cheer?" she asked.

Ron grinned. "Somebody's tweaked."

"Am not," Kim said—then she barked into

the Kimmunicator. "Wade! We need a ride!"

"What tweaked you?" Wade asked.

"I am *not* tweaked!" she barked again. *"Ride?"*

Wade pointed two thumbs toward the sky. The sound of a sleek hover jet filled the air.

Kim was amazed to see their ride appear so fast. "Wade, how did you get—?"

Then it dawned on Kim. "Oh," she groaned. The ride was Agent Will Du's.

Beep! Beep! Standing next to Kim, Will waved a tiny remote control in Kim's face. "The G.J. hover jet," he bragged. "Standard issue for all *top* agents."

The jet floated close to the ground. *Chachung!* Its metal door opened.

"Ladies first," Will said, rubbing it in.

Kim fumed, her arms crossed. "Thanks," she said, trying to be nice. But what she was thinking was definitely *not* nice.

CHAPTER 7

Killigan's Island

The hover jet zoomed across land and sea. Ron was the first to notice the tiny piece of rock surrounded by crashing waves. He pointed out the window. "There it is . . . Killigan's Island."

On the island sat a huge, old castle. It was totally "evil lair" material. Will parked the hover jet, and they all headed for the castle's front door.

"Killigan must want Professor Green to

49

build some kind of missile system," Will said as they entered the castle.

"I don't think so," Kim said. "Green's *green thumb* is the key to this."

"Yeah, okay, now see that door?" Ron pointed to a mammoth wood door at the far end of the castle hall. Torches burned on either side of it. "That just screams dungeon."

Both Will and Kim nodded. "Good call," they said.

As the three of them sneaked down the stairs, Kim tried to put it all together: "Killigan captures Professor Green. Then he buys a ton of hyperactic acid. Which, by the way, Professor Green had been experimenting with at his home."

Suddenly, Kim remembered something Wade had told her about Green. "Award-winning lawn!"

Ron raised an eyebrow and said, "You mean, the dude's invented some sort of super-grass?"

Just then, they realized something strange about this dungeon. The walls, the tables, the chairs . . . *everything* was covered in grass.

"Ron! Will! Quick!" Kim called from the other side of the dungeon. "I  found Professor Green!"

Actually, what she found was more like a big, man-sized clump of grass. Kim addressed the grassy clump. "Professor Green, are you all right?"

All they could hear were muffled groans. They had to do something, and fast.

Ron jumped to the rescue. "Hang on!" he yelled as he pulled out Rufus, whose teeth started chomping. Like a pair of clippers, Ron moved Rufus over the grass. *Chomp! Chomp! Chomp!* Soon the professor was free.

"Oh, thank you," the old professor said, coughing out all manner of pollen. "Killigan

trapped me in my own superfast-growing grass."

Kim gave Will an *I-told-you-so!* smile and said, "Supergrass. Huh? Really?"

Will, who was *not* smiling, shoved Kim to the side. "Professor Green, I'm Agent Will Du. We need to debrief on any weapons secrets that Killigan may have acquired."

The professor scratched his head. "Huh? Based on my work? Oh, Killigan could find out anything he wanted about my weapons work in a public library."

"Oh," said Will.

Score again! thought Kim.

Ron raised his hand and asked, "Bonus question: what does Killigan want to do with the supergrass?"

"Oooh, oooh, I know, I know!" At the top of the dungeon stairs, Duff Killigan was waving his hand, like a teacher's pet begging to be called on.

But it was Kim who got the answer: "Duff Killigan is planning on covering the world in grass. To create one giant golf course."

"My own personal golf course, lassie," Killigan hollered. He wore a tiny green beret and a loud plaid kilt.

And plaid is *so* last season, thought Kim.

"That's insane," Will said.

Killigan leaned forward to taunt Agent Du. "Oooh, just see if you get a tee time." Then Killigan darted away.

Will charged up the stairs, hoping to get a piece of Killigan. All he got was a dungeon door slammed in his face. He tugged hard on the handle, but the door was locked shut.

Kim walked up to the struggling Global

Justice agent. "Ah-uh-uh," she said. "*Ladies first.*"

She plucked a lipstick from her utility belt and pulled off the cap. *Zzzz!* This was no ordinary lipstick. This was a lipstick laser!

Kim sliced through the iron lock with her laser beam. She kicked the door open.

"I knew you were good, lassie," Killigan said, leaning against his golf bag in the middle of the room.

Suddenly, Will charged at Duff. But the sneaky Scotsman swiped a club under Will's feet.

"*Him* I'm not so sure about—" Killigan said, watching Will trip across the room and land in a heap.

Kim carefully approached the villain. "Mister Killigan, put down the golf clubs."

"You'll have to pry them out of my cold, dead hands," said Duff.

Out came another golf club. This time, Duff Killigan started whacking golf balls all around the room.

"Fore!" he screamed.

Kim jumped up, grabbed the chandelier, and swung safely out of the way. Will wasn't so lucky. Just as he started to wake up . . . *Whap!* He got it in the head with a stray ball. Agent Du was down again.

"Aw! What a beautiful slice!" Killigan

hopped up and kicked his heels in the air.

Kim flew down from the chandelier. She grabbed a pair of clubs from a wall ornament.

Duff became furious. "You ruined my coat of arms."

Kim twirled the clubs in her hands like a martial arts master. She said, "I'll put back what belongs to you when you put back what belongs to Professor Green."

Killigan pulled out two clubs and mimicked Kim's twirling moves. "I cannot do it. I've got plans for that formula."

Clash! Kim's clubs cracked the tops off

Duff's weapons. He pulled out his last two irons. *Clang!* Kim knocked the clubs from Killigan's hands.

"Oh, I'd love to play a round of Sudden Death," he said to her, "but I can't let the grass grow beneath my feet . . . yet." Killigan pushed a button on the fireplace, and a hole opened right below him. *Whoosh!* He fell through, and the hole closed again.

"Suddenly, the whole world is full of holes that people just whoosh away in!" Ron cried.

Will finally woke up. He rubbed his head.

Kim was already at the exit. "C'mon!" she called. "He's getting away!"

Outside, Kim pointed to the sky. "There he is!"

Will, Ron, and Professor Green all looked up. A huge blimp made of the same tacky plaid as Killigan's kilt floated away.

"We've got to get to the hover jet!" Will told the gang, Then, once again, he charged forward without thinking.

"Will! Wait!" Kim called as she, Ron, and the professor ran after him.

"What?!" cried Will. "He's getting away."

"You've gotta be more careful," Kim warned Will. "Killigan probably has the place booby-trapped."

"Try *sand*-trapped," Ron said when he noticed that everyone was slowly sinking . . . into quicksand!

CHAPTER 8

That Sinking Feeling

Kim, Ron, Will, and Professor Green sank deeper and deeper into the quicksand. They were now up to their necks, with their arms trapped by their sides.

"Okay, whenever you two are ready," Ron said to Kim and Will.

"What are you talking about?" Will growled.

"You *both* have a plan," Ron explained. "So, the sooner you guys fight over who has the *best* plan, the sooner we can get out of here."

"Your hover jet," Kim said to Will. "It must have a remote-command module or something!"

"Right. The R.C.M.," Will said, still sinking.

Ron grinned and said, "Kim shoots. She scores!"

Then Ron turned to Will and asked, "So where is this R.C.M.?"

Will frowned and said, "I, uh, left it in the hover jet."

Rufus, who was standing on Ron's head, put his head in his paws. "Oh!" He moaned.

That gave Kim an idea. "*Rufus* won't sink in the quicksand," she said.

With a snappy salute, Rufus hopped lightly down and tiptoed across the sand's surface.

Kim smiled proudly at Will. "Oh, I am *so* in the zone."

Will wrinkled up his face. "Impressive . . . for an amateur."

A couple of minutes passed. Ron began squirming in the sand. "This actually feels kinda nice," he said. Kim thought he was being a weirdo again. She wished Rufus would hurry.

Finally, Ron's naked mole rat returned—with the R.C.M. in his mouth.

Rufus spit the module at Will, who caught it in his teeth.

Through clenched teeth, Will said, "Nice work, rodent." He chomped down on the

R.C.M. *Beep! Beep!* The hover jet zoomed over to them. With another *beep! beep!* the hover jet dropped a rescue cable toward the quicksand.

"Ladies first," said Kim gleefully, making Will regret he'd ever used those teasing words on her.

As Kim was lifted out of the sand trap, Will said to Ron, "Why must she constantly irk me?"

"It's hard not to," Ron told him. "You're very irkable."

In no time, the hover jet was roaring through the air. Will was in the driver's seat. But his mind was not on driving. Instead, he turned all the way around to question Green. "Professor, did Killigan—?"

Kim grabbed Will's head and turned it back to the front. "You! Keep your eyes on the road."

With Will occupied, Ron decided to jump in. "So, Prof, any ideas about Killigan's target?"

"Oh, yes," Professor Green said, waving his arms around as he talked. "He intends to strike at the first country where he was banned from a golf course—Japan."

CHAPTER 9

Tokyo Attack

In Tokyo, Japan, frightened people ran through the streets screaming as a tidal wave of grass roared after them.

Behind it all, the evil Duff Killigan was tossing Professor Green's fast-growing seeds everywhere. A couple of sprinkles from his watering can of black-market fertilizer and *splort!* The grass erupted from the ground like a green, spewing volcano.

Killigan cackled madly. "It's pure dead brilliant!"

65

Will's hover jet arrived not a moment too soon. "Killigan! Stop!" Kim yelled, leaping to the ground.

"Nay! Not until the Pacific Rim is my driving range!" He threw seeds at Kim and drenched them with the supergrow liquid.

A huge surge of turf tumbled toward her. She jumped up and over the oncoming lawn. When she landed, it had already passed her by.

The hover jet was not so lucky. In a matter of seconds, the grass had completely covered the jet.

Inside, Will and Ron were trapped. Will pounded the dashboard and totally lost his cool. "Stupid, stupid, Will," he chided himself.

"Play it off, dude," Ron said. "Kim can handle the grass man."

"No. Prepare to eject," Will said and reached for the big, red EJECT button.

Punt! The ship ejected Will and Ron straight into the air. They flew right over the head of Duff Killigan.

Killigan ignored them. He was too busy driving a bunch of exploding golf balls at Kim. *Boom! Boom! Boom!*

A few yards away, Will landed coolly in a perfect crouch. But just as he was about to stand up, Ron flopped on top of him.

"Ow!" Ron cried, although he was glad Will had cushioned his fall.

Meanwhile, Killigan was raising a new club in the air. But before he could finish his swing, Will charged right up to him. He pushed the button on his standard-issue Global Justice stopwatch and . . . *flub!*

It didn't work.

Killigan stared at the broken watch—then he looked at Will. "Are ya daft, man?"

Ron peeked over Will's shoulder and said, "Maybe you gotta set it for local time."

Killigan finished his swing, sending the explosive ball high over Kim's head.

This guy? A pro golfer? Kim thought. *Hardly!* "Ha! You missed!" she yelled.

But Killigan had the last laugh. "It's a wedge, lassie. It's got backspin!"

Sure enough, the ball was still moving. Spinning on the ground, it was revers-ing—and head-ing straight for Kim!

She tried to run, but she couldn't escape. *Kaboom!* The explosion sent her flying.

She landed on a patch of grass. Dirt from the explosion rained down on her. This golfer had pushed her way past, peeved— Kim was in Total Tweaked City.

Then she saw something that made her

smile. "Heh!" she said, looking at a stray dandelion.

Duff Killigan stood over her with an evil scowl on his face. "Oh, you're in trouble now, lassie."

"No I'm not—you are," Kim said.

"And how would that be?" Killigan asked.

Kim bent down and plucked the dandelion. She waved it near his nose. "You've got dandelions."

Killigan sneered. "A wee weed. Bah!"

"Sure," said Kim, "but see every one of these little cottony things? They're seeds . . . every one of them."

Killigan was sweating, his voice hesitant. "Aye. So?"

"So, make a wish," Kim said as she blew on the flower. The little cottony seeds formed a cloud around the mad golfer.

He stood there, confused and nervous. He went cross-eyed, watching the one seed that landed on the tip of his nose.

Kim grabbed his watering can. *Splash!* She got him good.

"Aw, nah!" Killigan cried.

Fump! The weeds completely grew over the golfer. One by one, white dandelions popped out.

When Will and Ron ran over to join Kim, Duff Killigan had turned into *Fluff* Killigan— he was one big cottony ball of weed seeds.

"You're through now, lassie." Killigan spit

seeds out as he babbled on. "Get this weed out of me mouthie!"

Kim crossed her arms and smiled. She asked Ron and Will, "Should we have him arrested or *mowed*?"

Kim was joking, but Agent Will Du didn't get it. "I'll have G.J. send in a defoliation team."

"Or you could just give a neighborhood kid five bucks," Ron said.

"Humor. Amusing," Will said with a frown. Rufus, on the other hand, was laughing his naked mole rat head off!

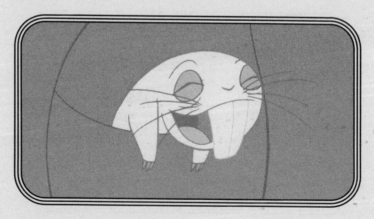

CHAPTER 10

A Final Thorn

now that Duff Killigan was trapped, Kim wanted to get back to the Bonnie Rockwaller problem. Saving the world from a rogue golfer? No big. But selling fund-raiser candy bars? That *was* a challenge.

She pushed Will toward his hover jet. "Okay, bye. Got to get home and have another thorn removed from my side."

"Oooh!" A strange, weedy yell came from

behind Kim. She turned to see Killigan leaping toward her.

Will snapped into position. He pushed the button on his stopwatch. This time it worked. *Zappo!* A shock ran through Killigan. He collapsed in a heap.

Will smiled. He had *finally* done something right!

Kim said, "Thanks. I've got to get one of those stopwatches."

Will lowered his head. For the first time, he wasn't acting like a brat. "Miss Possible, uh, Kimberly, I owe you . . . an apology."

"I'm glad you're a big enough person to admit it," Kim said.

Will grabbed Kim's hand and shook it, "You were of much assistance to me."

"Assistance?" Kim pulled her hand back. "Did you not pay attention to anything that happened?!" she cried in disbelief.

"Farewell, Kim Possible." Once Agent Will Du had the last word, he was gone.

Kim stood there with her mouth open. "I do not believe that guy."

Ron walked over

and listened to Kim spout off about Will. "He won't even consider that maybe somebody else deserves some credit," she said. "Maybe somebody else is as good as him."

"Maybe better," Ron said.

"Yes!" Kim was going full rant now.

Ron broke in. "We should get back to Middleton."

Kim kept going. "How hard is it to admit that somebody else is doing a great job?"

Ron put his hands on his friend's shoulder. "Seriously, Kim. We've gotta get back. You've got that whole Bonnie thing."

"Oh, and Bonnie—when will she just *give it up*?" Kim cried. "The fund-raising, the uniforms, the new cheer . . ."

"K.P.?" Ron interrupted.

"You're right, Ron. We've gotta go."

Back home, in the Middleton High gym, Bonnie Rockwaller stood in front of the other cheerleaders. All the cheerleaders were there. Well, all but one.

"Uh, I really think we should wait for Kim before we decide who's gonna be captain," Tara told Bonnie.

Bonnie threw a fit. "She's gonna be, like, forever. I want this captain thing decided *now*."

Just then, Kim and Ron walked into the gym. Kim wore her new uniform. The one that Bonnie had helped the team buy. "Relax, Bonnie," she said. "I'm back."

"Let's do it," Bonnie hissed.

"Fine by me." Kim turned to her teammates. All the way back from Japan, Kim had thought about what she would say to them.

She had thought about Will Du. He had wanted to be the number one agent so much  that he refused to give Kim any credit. And the mission was almost a big zero because of it.

Unless she wanted to act just like Will, Kim knew what she had to do. She took a deep breath and said, "I vote for Bonnie as the new captain."

The squad gasped! Bonnie was the most surprised of all. "You do?" Bonnie asked.

"Well," said Kim, "the fund-raising, the awesome uniforms, and that new cheer . . . I've gotta admit: you rock."

"Really?" Bonnie couldn't believe it.

Kim nodded, then asked in a big voice, "So, all in favor of Bonnie?"

Everyone responded with shouts of "Yay, Bonnie!" and "You go, girl!"

The team had found a new captain.

Kim congratulated Bonnie with a pat on the back. "You really worked hard for this."

"Yes," Bonnie said with an exhausted shrug of the shoulders. "Glad that's over."

"Bonnie, you're the captain now," Kim said. "You *do* realize that the hard work is just beginning?"

A look of horror crossed Bonnie's face. Her voice cracked. "You're kidding, right?"

Kim smiled. "You know, suddenly I couldn't be happier for you."

As Bonnie sulked out of the gym, Ron snapped her a salute. "Cap'n Bonnie!"

She ignored him. She was too busy thinking about what Kim had told her.

"I've gotta *keep* working hard," she groaned. "This is *so* unfair."

Ron whispered to Kim, "You countin' on the fact that she'll only last a month?"

Kim winked at her best friend. "I give her two weeks—tops."